BRATZ™

CHATZ

A Superstylin' Cyber Story!

YASMIN™
Pretty Princess

© MGA

JADE™
Kool Kat

© MGA

SASHA™
Bunny Boo

© MGA

CLOE™
Angel

© MGA

Used under license by Penguin Young Readers Group,
Published in Great Britain by Ladybird Books Ltd 2005
80 Strand London WC2R 0RL
A Penguin Company

10 9 8 7 6 5 4 3 2

Printed in Italy

LADYBIRD and the device of a ladybird are trademarks of Ladybird Books Ltd

A CYBER STORY TOLD IN SIX PARTS!

Part 1: YASMIN ™

© MGA

Okay, I *swear* it all started by accident. I mean, of course I've always got my senses extended to the max for a good story. After all, there are inches and inches of **blank space** in the *Stiles Shout-Out!* that have to be filled – and not just in my "Daily Doings" column (*plug, plug*).

I had just popped into the upstairs girls b-room for a gloss and powder touch-up before splitting school for the day. I decided to scoot down the back stairwell, rather than walk past the chem labs and their constant fog of **Experiments Gone Terribly Awry**. Anyway, the first thing I noticed in the stairwell was that it needed repainting, something that I was *definitely* going to mention in my next column. I mean, that stairwell goes all the way down to the basement, where the Maintenance Department has its offices. And the *whole* Maintenance Department troops up and down that stairwell every day. With all of that, you'd think that someone would have noticed that the stairwell needed work, **wouldn't you?** Then, while I was busy noticing that, I also noticed that there was someone singing down at the bottom of the stairwell.

You don't hear singing in the stairwell too often, so I gave it a listen. The acoustics were real sweet, and this **singer** was a nice tenor with a touch of hoarseness that kept it from being syrupy, if you know what I mean. It sounded like the guy was really dying of a broken heart and not just lip-synching the feeling. But the big surprise was *who* was doing the singing – *it was Dylan!*

Whoa, I thought, the boy was definitely **a star in the making**, and he was playing a fair acoustic guitar to back himself up. I was groovin' on his tones when the words suddenly sank into my brain and, like, I couldn't believe it! He was singing:

Prowlin' round with feline grace,
Kool Kat's the one that's settin' the pace.
Sleek and sassy, always dressed to kill,
She's the girl who makes my heart thrill.

Like I said, **I just couldn't believe it**, 'cause Kool Kat is Jade's nick, *right*? Dylan, crushin' on Jade? This was an ON THE SPOT EYEWITNESS FLASH that just *had* to be phoned in. I couldn't call and tell the girls about this, in case Dylan heard me, but I had two thumbs and that's why they invented text messaging. I flipped my cell and sent **SupR-scoop w/ fyrworkz! IM me when U get om!** to Jade, Cloe and Sasha. I lurked for a few more minutes, but all Dylan did was sing the same verse over and over, so I tiptoed back upstairs and bolted home for my laptop.

A half hour later, logged on and ready to chat, I checked my *Palz* list to make sure my gal pack was online and Instant Messaged them what I'd seen and heard. Jade was the first to respond, natch.

KOOL KAT:

OMG! Dylan's gr8, bt he's just my boy, my ace — my frNd!!! What hapnd? Did I snd some wrong signal or sumthin?

Sasha chimed in with:

BUNNY BOO:

Dunno. He's bin hangin' w Koby & all his techtoys 4 days now. Barely seen him.

Cloe, as usual, had the cute spin on things.

ANGEL:

Well, I think itz sweet. U could uz the boost a secret admirer brngz. Romance 4ever!

KOOL KAT:

G/f, I'm not so sure. Itz gonna tke me some time 2 wrap my brain round this. I mean, what hpns f it doesn't wrk out? do I lose him az a frNd?

I had to jump back in at this.

PRETTY PRINCESS:
Play it cool, like U alwys do. f itz meant
2 b, it will b.

ANGEL:
That's d groove! remembR, we'll alwys b
there 4 U, no m@R what. (((H)))

PRETTY PRINCESS:
Just 2 b sure, I'm gonna c f I can pry
more info out of Cameron & Koby. f Dylan's
crushin' on Jade, they'd know.

KOOL KAT:
bt will they tell U?

PRETTY PRINCESS:
I'm a reporter, babe, I have ways of
makin' men talk! :-D L8R.

I slid in at our table at lunch on Tuesday with the other girls already there. They looked great, as usual. I suppose I looked great, too, but I didn't feel great.

"'Sup, Princess?" Sasha asked.

"Zero. Zilch. Nada," I grumped. "I cornered Koby and Cameron this morning and dropped hints like birdseed around them, but they just ignored me. And when I came right out and asked if there was something 'special' going on with Dylan, they clammed up. The most I could get was that whatever *might* be going on – and they weren't saying that anything *was* – it was Dylan's private biz. So no exposé from me today."

"Don't be blue," Cloe said, as she passed me a sketch she'd just done. It showed me with a Sherlock Holmes hat and a half-dozen arms, holding a half-dozen magnifying glasses. Each hand had a hot shade of red or pink nail polish, of course. Signs all over the page pointed arrows different ways, each labelled, "SECRETS – THAT WAY." I smiled and added the sketch to the collection of Cloe's drawings I keep in my backpack. Someday, I'd use 'em to feature Cloe and other cool artists in my column.

Sasha winked at me. "Chill, girlfriend," she said. "While you've been getting the runaround, this Bunny's been hoppin'. **Dylan's secret is mine**."

Jade went ultrasonic. "And you didn't tell us?"

"I didn't say I had it *yet*," Sasha said. "Check it out. I'm supposed to drop by the A/V centre after school today. Koby promised he'd mix me some tapes from last weekend's rave. I guarantee that under the double influence of trance and chill-out, whatever he knows about Dylan is bound to slip out. I'll IM you at eight."

AWESOME ABBREVIATIONS!

Abbreviations are fast, fun, and totally now, and if you're gonna **IM, they're a must!**

Here are a few of our FAVOURITE ABBREVIATIONS.

Use 'em to **kick UP** the style of **YOUR** next IM convo!

© MGA

B	be	l8r	later
b/c	because	l%k	look
b/f	boyfriend	m@r	matter
b/w	between	n	in
b4	before	NE	any
bbl	be back later	NE1	anyone
brb	be right back	NEthing	anything
c	see	omg	oh my god
cu	see ya!	plz	please
ic	I see	r	are
f	if	ruok?	are you okay?
4	for	str8	straight
4ever	forever	2	two/to/too
g/f	girlfriend	2DA	today
gr8	great	2moro	tomorrow
h8	hate	u	you
in2	into	ur	your/you're
k	okay	u2	you too

Part 2:
JADE ™

I spent Tuesday afternoon **shopping** to keep my mind off Dylan and the whole relationship thing while I waited for eight o'clock to come. Funqué Junque, one of my **fave** vintage shops, had a whole new selection on display and I was in **heaven** as I collected silks and taffetas to restock my fabric trunks. In the back, I found an entire bucket of appliqué scraps that would provide me with accessorising bits for months. And **somebody, somewhere** had decided that an entire bolt of black lace just wasn't their thing, so I snatched it up for those outfits that could use a touch of Goth glamour.

Of course, buying stuff is only **half the job,** as I see it. Nothing's any use if you can't find it when you need it, you know? So I had to **budget** a couple hours for sorting and storing everything I'd bought. My walk-in closet is full of old shoe boxes and plastic boxes that I use to store all my cool fashion finds; it's so crammed that sometimes I think I should just SWITCH PLACES between my room and my closet, using the bigger space for storing my stuff and the closet for storing me!

Between doing all that and dinner, eight came around in a **flash**. As soon as I got back to my room, I revved up my computer and saw two IMs come in at once – Cloe and Yasmin asking me if I'd heard from Sasha yet. Before I could answer, Sasha logged in.

BUNNY BOO:
I'm here. Hold onto UR seats, b/c I've got a scoop, az pretty princess'd say.

KOOL KAT:
What did U find out frm Koby 2DA?

BUNNY BOO:
Itz not what I found out frm Koby, itz what I found while he wz out.

ANGEL:
Spill!!

BUNNY BOO:

Koby liked the mix he made so much he decided 2 burn it on CD. He left 4 a while & I found THIS piece of papR on the floor – n Dylan's hand-writing:

Pretty Princess has a Boho style,

A regal strut glidin' down the aisle.

On the street or in the school,

My royal doll was born to rule.

KOOL KAT:

I'm way confused now. 1st a luv song 2 me & now a luv poem 2 Yas? What's the boy playin' @?

ANGEL:

I think he's playin' the poor suffering artist, torn b/w 2 muses. He can't make ^ his mind who 2 devote himself 2. *S*. @--;----

BUNNY BOO:

Az much az Cloe luvs a romance & Yas luvs a mystery, I h8 a mess & this feels like sumthin I need 2 get str8. R U w me on this?

KOOL KAT:
What'd U have in mind?

BUNNY BOO:
2moro iz Wed... Dylan's last period iz free, just like Mon, so I'm figuring he'll b n the stairwell again. I'll stake it out 2 c f he's still singin' Jade's praises.

ANGEL:
Cameron's due ovr @ my place 2moro afternoon 2 do a kwik tune-up of my Cruiser.

BUNNY BOO:

Good. UR job iz 2 c f U can get NEthing out of him bout Dylan. Sweet talk him in2 lettin' sumthin slip. Yas?

PRETTY PRINCESS:

Yeah, g/f?

BUNNY BOO:

Stake out the A/V centre & Koby. Don't let on that I found NEthing, bt L%k 4 othR scraps of papR.

PRETTY PRINCESS:

Sasha's Angelz, on duty. :-*

BUNNY BOO:

IM rendezvous same time 2moro nite. K?

© MGA

We all agreed and after some more chat, we signed off.

Hours later, as I was getting ready for bed, I still didn't feel comfortable about Dylan's mixed messages to me and Yas. If I was feeling confused, how strange might Yas be feeling right then?

So I flipped out my trusty cell and sent her a quick text:

```
Yas. plz b ok.
txt me back asap.
```

I was in luck – she was still up. Her answer came back seconds later:

```
Dylan's bN weird. Don't let
it bug U. I still luv U no
m@R what.
```

I thumbed back:

```
good 2 know. BettR 2 hear.
BFz 2gether 4ever!
good nite.
```

She wrote back:

```
slp tight.
```

So I did.

KEYSTROKE ART!

Did you see that **rockin' rose** Cloe typed in our last **IM** sesh? We **love** making all sorts of cool art in our messages to one another. You do it just by using ordinary keys on your keyboard. Try it, and **express yourself** in a totally new way!

© MGA

```
@--;----                    rose

<3                          heart

<)                          slice of pizza

\_/7                        cup of coffee

|=------|                   bed

[{--Crayon--]}>             crayon  (feel free to use different colours)

=^..^=                      cat

< : 3 )~~~~                 rat

*<8-)X                      party outfit
```

Part 3: CLOE ™

© MGA

Wednesday was just **torture** for me. Even though I shared three classes and lunch with Dylan, I just couldn't look at him. Of course, I couldn't not look at him, *either*. I kept sneaking peeks at him. Didn't he know what he was **doing** to my **girlz**? Part of me wanted to scream at him, **"Why don't you just make up your mind?"**

After school, Cameron came by to tune up my **Cruiser**, lookin' all **cute** and serious as he leaned over the hood. But he kept his mouth shut about Dylan's secret. *What's with these boyz?*

I couldn't wait for the IM chat at eight, and I had to do something with all my energy after Cameron left. When I'm in a mood like that, I need to flex my **creativity** and my **muscles** at the same time. I can't do it with words, I've got to totally get down with my hands. There's nothing like **wedging clay** to burn calories and frustrations. I've got like twenty or so pounds of fine wet clay I keep in a sealed plastic bag in the garage. I took out enough to make a pot – about the size of a soccer ball – and started totally **slamming it down** on the wedging board I'd made the year before. You can't just shape and fire clay. It might have air pockets in it that'll for sure explode in the kiln and break anything else being fired. You have to slice it up against a stretched wire and slam it down on the board to knock out all the air bubbles. Wham! Wham! Wham! It's like a great upper body workout and it produces something totally ready to make art out of. By the time I'd finished, not only was I not feeling frazzled anymore, I'd decided to use the clay to make four fancy goblets, instead of a plain old pot – one goblet each for Sasha, Jade, Yasmin and me. A matched set, just like us.

I barely got cleaned up in time to chow down dinner and make it to my computer by eight. ON THE DOT, my girls were there.

BUNNY BOO:
We're all here. what have U got?

ANGEL:
k. I hung w Cameron while he tuned the FM Cruiser. Bo-ring! no str8 answers, bt he did admit that Dylan iz keepin' a secret. Not just frm us, bt frm everybody — the whole school. It's obvious that he knowz what it iz, & so duz Koby. bt they're not bout 2 spill 2 NE1.

PRETTY PRINCESS:
Koby knowz, alright. U had it lucky, Angel.
U were bored. I wz frustr8d hangin' n the
A/V centre. He wz mixing & taping sumthin
instrumental. He kept his headphones on all
the time & didn't once play thru the speakers so I could hear & groove along. A waste
of my time! :-(

ANGEL:
Sash?

BUNNY BOO:
well, I've got good news & bad news. The
good news iz that Dylan wz n the stairwell
again, & singin' again. the bad news ...
well, this iz what he wz singin':

Hip-hoppin' non-stoppin',
Play the music, she'll be boppin'.
Say it loud and say it true,
No one beats my Bunny Boo.

ANGEL:
Bt Bunny Boo iz U!

BUNNY BOO:
Yeah, I know.

PRETTY PRINCESS:

mAbE he knew U were ^stairs listenin' 2 him &
did it 2 tease U?

BUNNY BOO:

no, he wz really down w it by the time I
arrived & I didn't make NE sound. He didn't
know I wz there. I wz embarrassed.

KOOL KAT:

this iz way beyond mysterious. This iz totally
& uncharted Bzar.

BUNNY BOO:

K, let's get a grip here,
girlz. Let's all watch
the boyz closely 2moro.
We'll get the str8 story
frm them f NE1 can!

MORE IM SHORTHAND!

Here are some
more rockin' symbols
and abbreviations
to make sure you're
totally "up to speed"
when you IM with
your friends!

^	up
@	at
&	and
w	with
s	sigh
k	kiss
h	hug
aka	also known as
asap	as soon as possible
bf	best friend
btw	by the way
cmon	come on
f2f	face to face
fyi	for your information
gl	good luck
g2g	got to go
h/o	hold on
itz	it's
jk	just kidding
kit	keep in touch
lol	laughing out loud
nm	nothing much/never mind
ppl	people
qt	cutie
sry	sorry

sup?	what's up?
thx	thanks
tmi	too much information
ttfn	ta ta for now
w8	wait
wan2	want to?
wb	welcome back
wtg	way to go
wz	was
y	why?
yyssw	yeah yeah sure sure whatever
wysiwyg	what you see is what you get

Part 4: JADE™

Thursdays are **lonely days** for us girls. We have hardly any classes together and none in the afternoons this quarter. Still, it was fun playing **Sasha's Angels** all morning, spying on the boys and flicking our eyes away when they looked, so they wouldn't know we were **watching**. Sash kept **staring daggers** at Dylan, but he didn't notice. Don't boys know anything that's going on around them? Honestly, if it isn't TECH or it doesn't have a MOTOR or play on a team, the world is a BLANK to them.

Anyway, I was early to my World History class 'cause it's right next to my Comp Sci. class, when my phone buzzed. Getting phone messages between classes is risky, so I knew it **must be important.** I looked and saw a text message on my cell from Yasmin.

Dylan a×idntly cc'd me a msg he sent Koby & Cameron. IM me @ 3! MportNt!

I couldn't CONCENTRATE at all during my WH class, and I split the instant I heard **the bell,** so I could get home quick. My inbox already had an email from Yas, so I clicked it open.

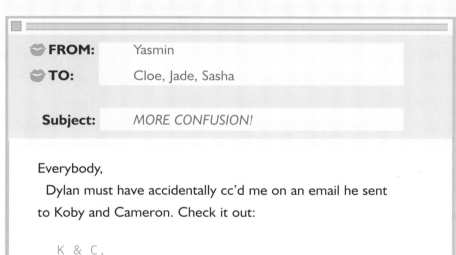

FROM: Yasmin

TO: Cloe, Jade, Sasha

Subject: *MORE CONFUSION!*

Everybody,
    Dylan must have accidentally cc'd me on an email he sent to Koby and Cameron. Check it out:

```
K & C,
How's this?

Gliding by in her halo of hair,
Angel makes my heart take to the air.
Got an assignment on the day of her birth
To make a little bit of heaven on Earth.

See U Fri afternoon.
                    D
```

The IMs started as soon as I
finished reading the email.

ANGEL:
That ... that's bout
ME! :-O!

BUNNY BOO:
Well, duh!

ANGEL:
This iz 2 much. We're not
boy-toys 4 him 2 play games
w. We have 2 face him down
bout this n the stairwell
2moro. U girlz w me?

© M●

This was a stunner. Cloe – sweet, gentle, romantic Cloe, who hardly ever gets mad at *anybody*.

PRETTY PRINCESS:
Nuh-uh. We can't confront the boyz n the stair-well.

ANGEL:
Y not?

BUNNY BOO:
R they on 2 us?

PRETTY PRINCESS:
My bad. I wasn't clear. what I meant 2 say wz that I sneaked a peek @ the A/V centre's schedule this afternoon & found out that Koby's booked the room 2moro's last period 4 – guess who? – Dylan!

BUNNY BOO:
Then we meet @ the A/V centre 2moro? >:-)

We all agreed and signed off.

EMOTICONS!

Now that things are heatin' up, emotions are flying! Talking online is always a blast, but at times like these, I'm always so grateful for emoticons. Even when I'm at a loss for words, I know I can express myself with these funky faces and every-one will know how I'm feel-ing. Here's a list of the hottest faces to use when you're expressin' **yourself** onscreen!

		=;	talk to the hand
		:-?	thinking
:-)	happy	<:-)	dunce
:-(	sad	L:-)	loser
:-*	kiss	>:-)	little devil
0:-)	angel	':-)	raised eyebrow
:-0	astonished	~:-o	baby
:,-(	crying	:-!	foot in mouth
:-D	laughing	(((H)))	big hug
I-0	yawn	]-)	wearing sunglasses
:"-/	embarrassed	:-(*)	makes me sick
@:-)	just got back from the hairdresser	:0)	clown
		>_<	ouch!
:-P	teasing or drooling	>:-(	angry
		%-(	confused
		:-/	disappointed

Part 5: SASHA ™

We must have looked like the Fashion Army on patrol when we met in front of the A/V centre door on Friday. Since we were heading for a showdown, we made sure we were dressed to kill. I took the lead and hammered on the door, hard – I had to, since the A/V centre is soundproofed so they can do recordings in there – but even through the soundproofing, we could hear a throbbin' bass line. They were playing *something* on speakers in there. Eventually, the bass line stopped and Koby opened the door. He blinked when he saw us.

"Um . . . hi," he said, standing in the doorway. "Sorry, this is a private session."

Cloe surprised all of us by pushing in ahead. "It became *our* business when Dylan started writing about *all of us*," she said hotly.

That crumpled Koby and he backed up as the rest of us followed Cloe into the lab. Dylan sat on a stool at the far end of the lab, headphones on his ears and leaning in toward a mic covered with a red wind baffle that looked like a clown nose. He looked stunned when we all piled in. Cameron, in his usual jeans and oversized tee, sat tilted back in a chair with his trainers propped up on the corner of the soundboard. He nearly fell on the floor at the sight of us.

Cloe snaked past Cameron and shoved some papers into Dylan's hand. It must have been the four "love poems" or whatever they were that we'd found out about that week. **"Wanna explain these?"** she demanded.

I swear I nearly lost it when Dylan actually *blushed* at Cloe. Cameron's and Koby's jaws dropped, then all three boyz fell over on themselves laughing. *What did they find funny about all of this?*

Cameron got his cool back first. He slouched back in his chair and locked his fingers behind his head. "Might as well fess up, D," he drawled. "They're on to you, and we can't keep your secret forever, you know."

"Okay, okay," Dylan said with a grin. "But I'm not sure where to start . . ."

Yasmin jumped in. "We know *why* you're so confused, because we're all so amazin' . . ."

"Yeah," I added. "It's sweet and all that you're crushin' on all of us, but . . ."

"Which one of us do you really love?" demanded Jade. The four of us stared hard at Dylan.

Cameron, Koby and Dylan hit the floor laughing again.

"Wait, wait . . ." Dylan said as he recovered. "Don't fight over me, ladies." He ran his fingers through his hair, preening like a peacock. "I know I'm hard to resist, but I don't love any . . ."

© MGA

Cameron made car-alarm noises. Koby barked, "Danger, bro! Danger! Foot heading for mouth! Cancel! Cancel!"

We looked at them in complete and utter mystification. Then Cloe said what was on all our minds: "What in the world is so funny?"

At that, Dylan straightened up and shot a frustrated look at his pals, who were still howling. "I'm just trying to explain . . ."

"Why explain?" Koby said. "Just play the tape." He jabbed a button on the board.

A **strong bass** run filled the room from the four speakers mounted in the corners of the lab. In spite of myself, my foot began tapping to it, followed by my hips and then my fingers. A sweet, tripping keyboard kicked in, sprinkling licks as the music found its groove and started to build. I was watching Dylan. His **blush** was **deepening**, and when his voice suddenly came on the speakers, *I knew why*. Not that he was bad, just that he had an unexpected audience. His recorded voice sang:

PROWLIN' ROUND WITH FELINE GRACE,
KOOL KAT'S THE ONE THAT'S SETTIN' THE PACE.
SLEEK AND SASSY, ALWAYS DRESSED TO KILL,
SHE'S THE GIRL WHO MAKES MY HEART THRILL.

PRETTY PRINCESS HAS A BOHO STYLE,
A REGAL STRUT GLIDIN' DOWN THE AISLE.
ON THE STREET OR IN THE SCHOOL,
MY ROYAL DOLL WAS BORN TO RULE.

The bass line skipped into a complex hip-hop rhythm as the keyboard faded back. Then Dylan's voice kicked in again, **stronger**, with pops and scratch-sounds until he was ready with the next verse.

© MGA

HIP-HOPPIN' NON-STOPPIN',
PLAY THE MUSIC, SHE'LL BE BOPPIN'.
SAY IT LOUD AND SAY IT TRUE,
NO ONE BEATS MY BUNNY BOO.

The keyboard returned with a heavy run of power chords and a blistering synth lead solo. No bridge, but a flat-out climb and crescendo that shook the room before returning to the original arrangement. Dylan came in again.

GLIDING BY IN HER HALO OF HAIR,
ANGEL MAKES MY HEART TAKE TO THE AIR.
GOT AN ASSIGNMENT ON THE DAY OF HER BIRTH
TO MAKE A LITTLE BIT OF HEAVEN ON EARTH.

The music faded to a silence I was afraid to break.

"It's a *song!*" Cloe breathed. She ran up and hugged Dylan. "How sweet!"

That was enough to turn Dylan from sunburnt to a **beet**.

"What's it for?" I asked.

"Spill," Yasmin said, whipping out her notebook and starting to write. "This is going on page 1 of the *Stiles Shout-Out!*"

Dylan hemmed and hawed, but finally started talking. "Well, KMZIK has been having a songwriting contest for the town, you know. Koby wanted to test his chops producing a song, and I've always wanted to write and sing. And Cameron..." He jabbed a thumb at his friend, who was smirking. "... is always ready to lend a hand supervising what **somebody else is already doing.**"

"You gotta go with your strengths," Cameron offered.

"Anyway, I couldn't come up with anything for the longest time," Dylan said. "Everything I wrote was lame, or just plain fake-sounding. Good songs have to have a core of truth to them, you know?"

© MGA

He was really **warming** up to his topic. We could tell that he was seriously down with doing it right. "I wanted to do something with **feelings**, like a **love song**, but I'm not hooked up with anyone, so . . ." he trailed off. "But then, I thought about the four of you. I mean, you're all **special to me**, and you're all so **different**. I suddenly wanted the **world** to know about you so that they could appreciate you as much as I do. After that, the verses just wrote themselves as I played in the . . ."

". . . stairwell in the back of the school," Yasmin interrupted, still scribbling madly in her notebook. "**That's** where I heard you earlier this week."

"You were listening to me **practice**?" Dylan squeaked.

He looked so **embarrassed**, we all had to laugh. "Yeah," I put in. "Then we started finding all these **clues** everywhere – a verse you left here in the A/V centre . . ."

"And the verse you **accidentally** cc'd me when you emailed these guys," added Yasmin.

"Well, I think it's all **perfectly romantic**," insisted Cloe.

"So you like it?" Dylan asked hesitantly. "I mean, *all of you?*"

"I give it a 12 out of 10," I said. Jade and Yasmin nodded in agreement.

"Cool," said Koby, impressed.

The song's rhythms were still rocking in my head. I wanted to hear it again. Shoot, I wanted to get down and *dance* to it! Still, I couldn't resist one little jab for all of the twists the boys had put us through. "Unfortunately, there's just one thing missing from the song that keeps it from being **perfect** . . ." I said.

Dylan, Cameron and Koby exchanged worried looks. "What's that?" Dylan asked.

I looked at Cloe, Yasmin and Jade. We are such good friends that sometimes we can almost read one another's minds. "A girl backup chorus!" we said in unison.

© MGA

It was a good thing the A/V centre was **soundproofed**, or the whole school would have come running to see why seven people were **laughing** so hard.

WHAT TYPE OF IM GIRL ARE YOU ?

When you're online with your friends, it's all about **expressin' yourself**! You may not realise it, but your IMs are filled with **information** about how you like to express yourself. With every word you type, your **awesome** personality comes SHININ' THROUGH! To find out your gabbin' online **inner self**, take this quiz!

1 **When talking to your BFFs online do you:**

   a. Respond immediately?

   b. Take your time and come up with the most thoughtful answer?

   c. Forget to respond?

   d. Type the fewest words possible to get the point across?

2 **In F2F conversation, your friends would describe you as:**

   a. A fast talker

   b. A great listener

   c. A little spacey

   d. A woman of few words

3 How many hours do you spend online a day?

a. Four fast-paced, drama-filled hours where the fingers (and gossip) fly

b. An hour-long conversation with one of your galpals about your most delicious crush

c. You have no idea – your computer's on, but you're never there

d. Ten minutes, and you have ten conversations at the same time

4 If you find you can't stand talking to one of your girls online, is it because:

a. She takes too long to respond?

b. She talks for two minutes and then signs off?

c. Come to think of it, she never IMs you anymore

d. She doesn't understand your abbreviations?

5 Your typical online good-bye sounds a bit like:

a. Bye Girl (Enter)
See ya tomorrow (Enter)
Love Ya (Enter)

b. I'll see you tomorrow. Remember we have that killer exam in science, so get a good night's sleep. I had a super-cool time dishin' with you tonight!

c. You don't say good-bye. Instead, you return to your computer after going to the gym or watchin' a kickin' TV show to see that everyone else has signed off.

d. L8R G8R

If you picked mostly a's...

You're a turbo-fast typist, 'cause you can't wait to get those thoughts out of your head! You love talking – online or off – and you're fun, funny, and have a kickin' online style. You always have a comeback and you're never at a loss for words. It wouldn't be surprising if your zodiac sign was Aries, Leo or Sagittarius – all fire signs. Fire signs argue with passion. Fires move as they please, girl, so go with the flow!

If you picked mostly b's...

You're a slammin', thoughtful "IM-er." When people need to talk, they come to you. You're compassionate, warm and always think before you speak. It's not that you don't have anything to say; it's just that you want to say it *correctly*. It's a good guess that you are a Taurus, Virgo or Capricorn – earth signs. You're somewhat of a perfectionist – always searching for that ideal response. But don't let all that fool ya; earthy girls are the chillest divas in the zodiac.

If you picked mostly c's...

You are an unpredictable chatter. You don't mind being online, but you just can't sit still. Sitting by a computer all day is a total yawn for you. Go where the wind takes you, girlfriend. You're the greatest friend offline, and everyone understands that you just don't have time to type when you're always moving. You are probably a water sign – Cancer, Scorpio or Pisces. You change what you're doing easily, but you're radiant at everything you do!

If you picked mostly d's...

Sup, g/f? U use more abbreviations than NE1 else on your buddy list – most people can't even keep up with U! U pride URself on being in and out of a convo in less than 5 min. It's not that U don't love talking online, it's just that you have so many people 2 talk 2. How can a rockin' girl keep up without using the hippest language out there 2DA? You're most likely an air sign – Gemini, Libra or Aquarius. U think fast and use words and phrases in original ways all the time. It's not that U use online slang – U *created* it!

Part 6: YASMIN™

Well, Dear Reader, that's exactly how it all happened. Except for our last IM session on the topic that night, that is.

© MGA

PRETTY PRINCESS:
Every1 here?

BUNNY BOO:
Yo!

KOOL KAT:
=^..^=

ANGEL:
0:-)

PRETTY PRINCESS:
wz this the wildest week we've eva had or what?

BUNNY BOO:
Yeah, thx 2 our ace reporter. "News flash: boyband wnab falls n luv X 4 — or writes song. Film @ eleven."

PRETTY PRINCESS:
Hey, I wz only followin' a lead.

KOOL KAT:
& L%k where it led us.

ANGEL:
The important thing iz that we're all still 2gether.

BUNNY BOO:
2gether 4eva.

KOOL KAT:
All 4 1 & every1 4 the mall!

PRETTY PRINCESS:
U got it. nite, gang. luv U all. :-*

XOXO,

YASMIN™
@--;-----
Pretty Princess

JADE™
@--;-----
Kool Kat

SASHA™
@--;-----
Bunny Boo

CLOE™
@--;-----
Angel